For Penny – F.S.

For Marah – E.O'N.

**SIMON & SCHUSTER**
First published in Great Britain in 2022 by Simon & Schuster UK Ltd
1st Floor, 222 Gray's Inn Road, London WC1X 8HB
Text copyright © 2022 Frances Stickley • Illustrations copyright © 2022 Eamonn O'Neill
The right of Frances Stickley and Eamonn O'Neill to be identified as the author and illustrator of
this work has been asserted by them in accordance with the Copyright, Designs and Patents Act, 1988
All rights reserved, including the right of reproduction in whole or in part in any form
A CIP catalogue record for this book is available from the British Library upon request

ISBN: 978-1-3985-0894-1 (HB) • ISBN: 978-1-3985-0893-4 (PB) • ISBN: 978-1-3985-0895-8 (eBook)
Printed in China • 10 9 8 7 6 5 4 3 2 1

# NOT A CAT IN SIGHT

**FRANCES STICKLEY**          **EAMONN O'NEILL**

**SIMON & SCHUSTER**

London   New York   Sydney   Toronto   New Delhi

Mouse was feeling fabulous.
The sky was blue and bright.
The day was warm and wonderful,
with **not** a cat in sight.

No whiskers in
the wardrobe.

No scratching at
the door.

No paws.
No purr.
No balls of fur.

No catnip on the floor.

*A perfect day to dream*, thought Mouse.
*A perfect day to play.*
*Imagine what could happen*
*on a day just like today.*

"Roll up for the circus!"
cried the mighty little mouse.

"And see me scale the tightrope
as I hop from house to house!"

He teetered and he toppled
and he squeaked with sheer delight . . .

as he walked along the washing line
with **not** a cat in sight.

"Or better yet, a skydiver!
And ready,
steady . . . go!"
Mouse prepared his parachute and cried,

# "Geronimo!"

He leapt and laughed and marvelled
as he suddenly took flight . . .

and he landed in the compost heap
with **not** a cat in sight.

"**But wait!**" cried Mouse.

"What's under here?

A jewel from long ago?

A diamond or

a treasure chest?

A golden crown or . . . oh.

It's just a bone," he sighed,
and pulled it up
with all his might . . .

then raced towards the garden pond
with **not** a cat in sight.

"Perhaps I'll be a pirate!
Call me Captain Squeaky Paws!
But, avast! Beware, me hearties,
there be sharks in these 'ere shores!"

He rode a wayward whale, though it put up quite a fight . . .

as they tumbled over ocean waves
with **not** a cat in sight.

*I could be a bird,*
thought Mouse,

*and* **soar** *across*
*the sky.*

Just floating on a cloud

as all the world passes me by.

*And all the Earth beneath me*
*seems so far away and small.*

On such a lovely day,
I could be anything at all.

When the world is fine and fabulous,

the sky is blue
and bright . . .

. . . and the day is warm

and **wonderful** . . .

. . . with **not** a cat in sight.